A DAFFY DIARY

QUOTES AND MICRO FICTION

ARQAM BAZMY

To my mother Dr Neelofar without whose never ending love, encouragement and trust I would have taken another three years to complete this book.

Contents

A few thousand copies sold can make an author successful but the real success lies in the inner satisfaction.
Real sign of intelligence is neither education nor qualification.
It's just imagination.
To become a good writer you must become a great dreamer first.
When poets and mountains meet, legends are composed.
Life is not just about living.
Death has its own mysteries to unfold.
I finally found my home in the hollow of your hand.
It is my poetry that saves me from slaughtering humans.
Be the kind of person you wish to meet, you wish to see, you admire, and you finally fall in love with!
Your pain becomes the cure once you stop feeling it.
I never tried to fit in because I knew it from the beginning that I was born to stand out.
I like to take things slow because I am a writer and writers are the masters of patience and observation.
You are the only person who really knows what you actually want.

Listen to your heart and follow your heartbeats. They'll definitely take you to your desired destination.

She is like a mug of coffee.

A little sweet, a bit bitter, served hot, brewed to the perfect temperature, poured into a ravishing mug with the topping of cream.

She is the perfect one.

Trees make me believe in the fact that one must change his colour with the changing seasons.

Cats do speak but only to those who lend them their ears.

As a child my ambitions kept changing every day. At a time I wanted to become a pilot, a doctor, a journalist' a scientist, an entertainer, a bureaucrat and there was a time when I even wanted to become an environmentalist.

Hence, I finally became a writer.

Life is all about ups and downs.

Ever seen an electrocardiogram?

Stability is just another figure for death.

Sometimes I wake up and find myself in a mood of no human interaction.

The only things I care about are my fantasies, dreams, stories, poetry and pen.

My sole purpose in life is to sleep, dream and come up with a fantasy that the world has never heard of.

Sunlight crawls into my room like it would never fade away and fades away as it would never visit again.

A poet's charm stands above every other charming thing in this world.

The silence of the night is warm and peaceful when after a day full of chaos and distractions, people can finally dream, sleep, write or drown into the memories of their loved ones.

Take me to a place where the sky touches the earth, where the raindrops dance, where the sun peeps out of a curtain of clouds scattering the warmth of comfort and where the dying souls are resurrected to life.

When I run out of ideas,
I simply steal them...

I don't like small talk.

I like long conversations about life- the meaning of life, the purpose of life, the love of life, the light of life and death.

I always welcome winter with a smile, a hot brewing mug of coffee served with a fantastic story, a quilt and some delicious food.

Never cook a delicious story unless you know whom to serve it.

In my morning walks, I look for the sun arising from the heart of the earth, the warm sunlight glittering all over the plants, trees, grass, roads and buildings, the moist dew fading away with sunlight, starting a new chapter of life and death.

Life is truly lived only when you let your soul exit your body to dance among the twinkling stars and wander with the floating clouds.

The night never waits for your soul to exit your body and dance in the moonlight. You must gather all your courage and find that one soul with whom you wish to dance all night.

When my family comes together,
a unique constellation is formed which depicts eternal love, strength and a fairy tale.

O Love! I set you free
from the shackles of love
to let you dance in bright sunshine

and learn to love the ones who love you.

Poets take care of the society in a way which the governments can never afford to.

The sunlight crawls into my house like a snake and coils around every object to squeeze the dullness out of them.

In this city of dreams,

a dream is shattered every second and a poet is born to dream.

Men built a city and a poet turned it into the city of dreams.

I miss you like the dark clouded nights long of a glimpse of the moon.

Leaving home feels like abandoning your favourite pair of shoes and wearing a pair that doesn't fit you but you are told that they would fit you fine with the passage of time.

Dear Men!

You are the best creatures on this land. Just accept what you are.

Don't try to step in anyone else's shoes.

From Adam to Mohammed, you have been the messengers of peace and have given this world a thousand reasons to live.

You are the best when you are pious and the worst when you are evil.

You are just incomparable.

When I wake up earlier than usual, I find the whole world greeting me with open arms.

The sun showers the sunlight, the wet meadows pave a soft way for my feet. The sky keeps changing colours from dull to bright. The flowers smile and blush at my touch.

What more can a poet want from life?

If I were to write an autobiography, it will be called-

"The death of a man and the rise of a poet."
Let your soul fly away like a flying dove,
When you feel those flapping wings,
You'll understand the meaning of love.
It's only with friends that the best pages of your life are composed or decomposed.
Call me an anarchist if you want to but
Cleanliness for me means a nation clean of politicians.
Loneliness feels like a chance to interact with the best and worst of yourself.
This world is in search of more poets and artists, not politicians.
How to become a writer?
To become a writer, you need to learn the art of smearing ink on paper with fantasies, dreams, desires, magic, words and ideas.
Life is incomplete until the emergence of death.
Nights aren't meant for just sleeping or dreaming.
They are meant to let your soul fly away and bathe is the milky moonlight and then air it under the shadow of the twinkling stars.
You sometimes ought to be a warrior to ultimately be an ambassador of peace.
Nights make me believe that sometimes a dim light and dullness can be more scenic and beautiful than bright sunshine.
Life is a mixture of some bitter beans and a little sugar.
Cream toppings are a matter of choice.
Life is just a perfect mug of coffee.
A poet is born to appreciate every beautiful thing which the world never cared to look at.
I wish dreams were promises, so the moon could sit beside me and watch the twinkling stars all night.

Life surprises us the most only when we let it slip from our hands and expect the least from it.

If my mirror could speak, it would be crying out loud with a thousand new mouths.

I can't forget how I was abused, raped and murdered again and again for raising my voice to prove my existence.

Don't write until words come bursting out of your pen to beat the shit out of this world.

Don't ever ask me to stop dreaming because I live in a different dream every time I breathe.

When I look at the mirror, I see an idiot who is born to dream.

The most important thing in life is to dream and share those beautiful dreams with the rest of the world.

Once upon a time there lived a ghost.

He used to haunt people and was pretty good at it.

Then one day, the politicians arrived.

The ghost retired for good.

The journey has come to an end.

I can't feel those butterflies flying even when I have you in my arms.

Loving yourself is not about keeping yourself safe and sound.

It is about risking yourself to such extend that makes you either extinct or a legend forever.

Falling in love for the first time feels like living in a beautiful dream where you are just so scared to open your eyes.

Tonight, I feel like writing.

I wish the writer inside me bleeds to death.

Life is made up of two components-

Smiles and tears.

The way I look at you

is far better and romantic than
the way you look at me.
Having you in my life is like the sight of a full moon in the sky filled with millions of twinkling stars.
Late nights have never been such an inspiration before.
As the sky turns dark, I start turning into an old wise owl equipped with the finest thoughts and the rarest dreams in the world.
One scary thing that didn't seem scary when I did, was fall in love.
A fool is not someone who accepts the fact that he is one,
But someone who is always trying to prove himself a genius.
Nobody is born to live here.
Everybody just breathes in and out and finally breathes out.
You are the kind of fire which enlightens my soul.
You are the light of my life.
If only love was as strong as hatred,
I would still have been a human being.
Memories without a picture are like a piece of poetry without words,
embedded somewhere deep in your heart.
I come from the land of humans where practicing and believing in magic is forbidden.
During the times of global lockdown, due to the pandemic,
"she" who was not with her man was missing him like hell and "She" who was locked down with her man was behaving in a manner that clearly expressed that her man was the most frustrating thing in the world.
Understanding "her" is indeed an impossible task.

I often forget my responsibility towards the society as a writer, but every now and then some idiots keep reminding me of it.

Behind every successful man, there is always a shy introvert boy buried deep down.

To love life,

You need to truly understand the concept of death.

Love is the master of all other emotions in this world.

Black is the colour of the background of almost every beautiful thing in this world.

If words had fragrance,

then I would have been a great perfume maker who is allergic to his own perfumes.

The city is lit.

But the corner where I live outshines the whole city.

The moon spent last night sitting on my lap.

When I look at my past, I see a huge pile of mistakes I committed and I am thankful to them as they made me what I am today.

The little bit of light that comes in my house is the light of your heart and

that light is the light of my life.

"what is more important-

a luxurious life

or

a peaceful death?", he asked?

She smiled and said, "I don't care because I shall die in your arms."

They say death.

I hear peace.

End of story.

Hunger tastes like nothing.

It's just an abstract form of mixed emotions.

A friend: I am so tired. The burden on my shoulders is too much to bear.
Me: Let that burden fall away. Smile and give this world a chance to admire the most lovely portrait ever painted by the almighty himself.
The air carries your smell.
I can feel your fragrance tinkling my alveoli. I am back into my kingdom of fantasies and dreams.
I start falling in love once again.
Then, I just put on my face mask and walk away.
Prosperity is the luxury that has never been achieved by a human being in the history of mankind.
I believe that my words are eternal as they address mankind.
She was happy.
I was not.
Then a drop of tear from my eye fell upon her pall.
My journey towards you began when the whole universe was at my side.
The closer I came to you, one by one everyone else walked away.
But I still feel the whole universe is with me.
Writing isn't about the quantity of ink smeared on a piece of paper.
Writing is all about playing with the reader's emotions, thoughts, imagination and existence.
Dear boys!
Before you turn into men,
try to feel the woman inside you; so that when you encounter one you know how to react.
We are socialists.
We don't discriminate even between day and night.
We sleep all the time...

Your silence can sometimes snatch away your innocence.

Cry out loud if you need to, so that you remain an innocent child for the rest of your life.

Some people just date a single person and find their soulmate.

Then there is a category of idiots like me who prepare for a new audition every month.

Take me to a place where the mountains live among the clouds, where the earth kisses the sky, where there is no room for politics, revolution or civilization.

Where there is just beauty, poetry and love...

I would rather die than leave that place.

My expressions are a mere reflection of my suffering, exploitation and imagination.

I am something which is a little more than a mirror.

Know that, racism and bigotry have no place in your world which is already occupied by poets and dreamers like me.

Love doesn't stay where
you wish to stay forever.

What might be life for someone
is just a story for me
and vice versa.

What is time?

Time is something worth wasting so that realise its value.

Would you believe if I tell you that I am a writer and I never tell lies.

I like to spend the night dreaming about those things which I can't achieve during the day.

You must at least pretend to be alive, until death comes knocking on your door.

I desire to see you again and again.
Coffee is just a lame excuse.
Life is not a marathon.
Its just a huge collection of a hundred metre sprints.
The day is the same but today the sky looks more pink than usual.
Just like the full moon,
I'll too fade away some day.
To write a good story,
You must read a thousand great stories first.
The moon told me a story,
and I composed a poem out of it.
When I speak, I just speak.
But when I write,
I cry, I laugh, I sing and dance, I live and I finally die when I can't write anymore.
I am not afraid of death.
What really frightens me is this life.
You still think of her because she never gave a fuck about you.
Boys try to change a girl.
Men change their direction.
Life wouldn't be worth living if death was not the end of it.
At the end of a long journey,
those ten seconds of happiness make you realise that
destination is something that really doesn't matter.
It's always the journey that makes the trip memorable.
You touched me, and suddenly all that poetry started to make sense.
Years of great sex do not promise an everlasting relationship because when the passion settles down, what is left?

Rebels are rare.
Sycophants are everywhere.
All men are idiots.
And women claim that they aren't any lesser than men.
When I spend time with myself I realise how important and resourceful I can be to myself.
Try to live the life that you love but love the life that you live.
This is your key to happiness.
Trust me.
Spirituality and love are the diet for your soul.
Keep your soul not just alive but healthy too.
When I look at the birds in the sky,
I wonder how it must feel to freely fall from the sky and still not break a single bone.
The night is trying to draw the map to the greatest achievements of your life in the near future.
I fell for you
when then whole world was falling down on me.
What we may never achieve individually,
can definitely be achieved by a community.
Why just exist in this exceptionally beautiful world where you can live your life to the fullest.
Be a person who is not afraid of loneliness because the darkest secrets of life are revealed to you only when you are lonely.
Everything you write is a piece of art until you start reading those branded writers.
A few drops on the leaf asked me if I could save them from vanishing with the first rays of sunlight.
You'll never know how helpless I felt at that moment.
Try to write something that slides though the eyes and settles down deep in the heart.

"Magic is a lie", exclaimed someone from the audience.
"And so is your existence", replied the magician.
It isn't the size of the audience that decides the quality of the show.
It's the happy faces of the audience at end that tell you that the show must go on.
She cried out loud," My beauty shall soon fade away. My warm pink lips shall someday become cold and white. My big black eyes shall soon be dull and nobody would even care to look at me."
He gently replied," Try to fall in love with a poet and this shall never happen to you."
She sold herself tonight to pay for her son's school fee.
"You are a whore. It would have been better if I were an orphan than having a mother like you." the son roared and threw those folded currency notes at her face.
She picked up the money and tucked it in her blouse with great difficulty.
Tears rolled down her eyes.

A Succesful author

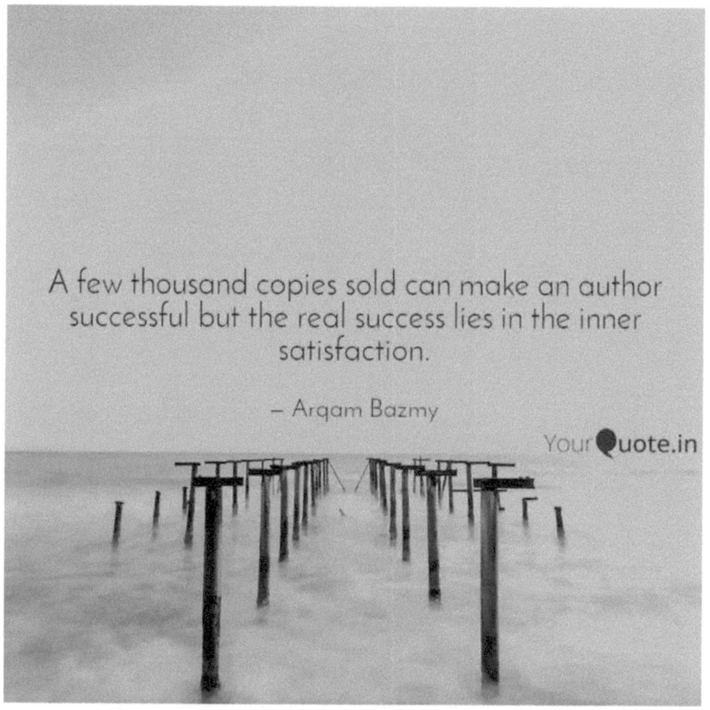

Enter Caption

The Genius

Enter Caption

How to become a good writer?

Enter Caption

Why should I write?

Enter Caption

Printed by Libri Plureos GmbH in Hamburg,
Germany